This bedtime story belongs to:

....

Goodnight, Rolo. Sleep well.

First published in Great Britain in 2018 by Hodder and Stoughton
This paperback edition published in 2018

Author photo by Adam Bronkhorst

Hodder Children's Books
An imprint of Hachette Children's Group
Part of Hodder and Stoughton
Carmelite House
50 Victoria Embankment
London, EC4Y 0DZ

Hachette Ireland
8 Castlecourt
Castleknock
Dublin 15, Ireland

ISBN 978 1 444 95677 1

1 3 5 7 9 10 8 6 4 2

Printed in China

An Hachette UK Company
www.hachette.co.uk

Hodder
Children's
Books

Goodnight, Mr Panda

Steve Antony

I am going to bed.
Goodnight, Mr Panda.

You've forgotten to brush your teeth.

I'll brush them
twice in the
morning.

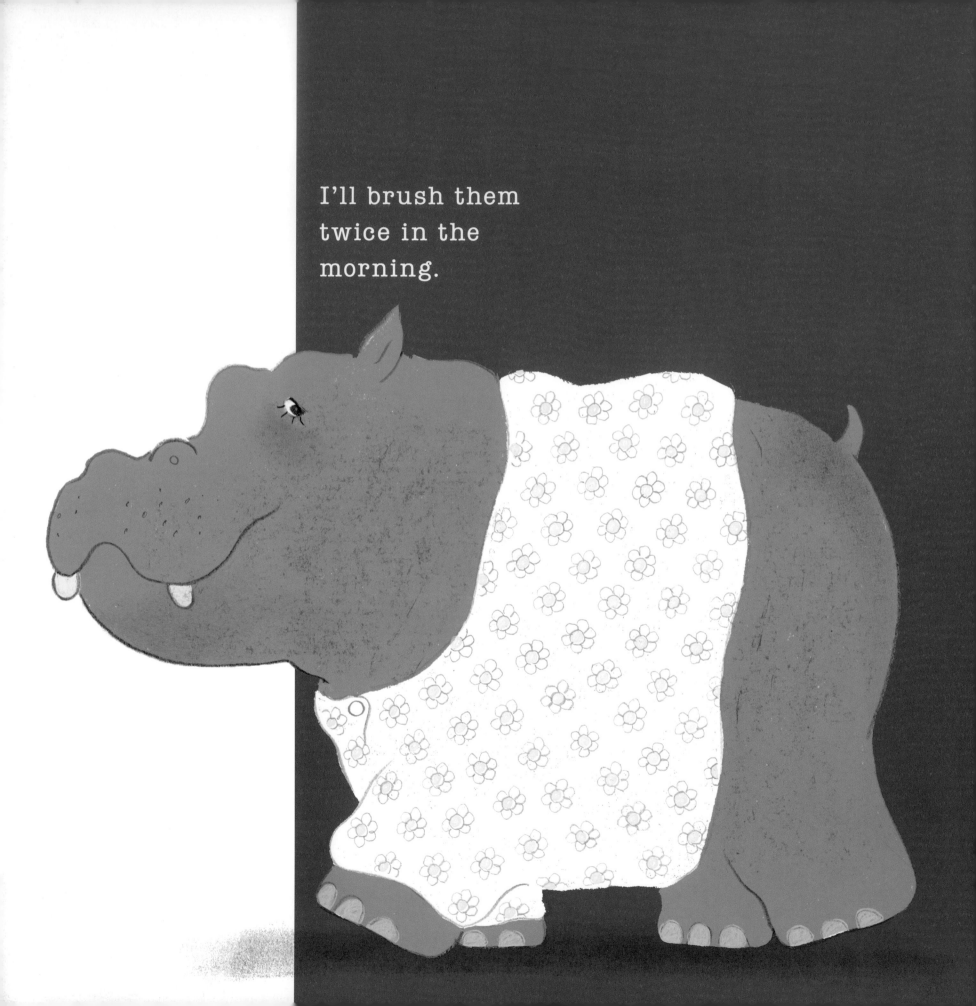

My mouth is minty fresh!

Goodnight, Hippo.

I'm going to bed, too.
Goodnight, Mr Panda.

You've forgotten to have a bath.

But I had
a bath
last year.

I'm
as
fresh
as
a
daisy!

Goodnight, Skunk.

You should go to bed, Sloth.

I'm too tired to move.

We are going to bed. Goodnight, Mr Panda.

You've forgotten
your pyjamas.

Sheep don't
wear pyjamas.

Goodnight, Sheep.

But lemurs do!

Mr Panda, are you
going to bed?

Yes.

Haven't you
forgotten
something?

Goodnight, Lemur.

Goodnight, Mr Panda.

But Mr Panda...

...that's my bed!

More fantastic books from
Steve Antony...

Thank You, Mr Panda
Steve Antony

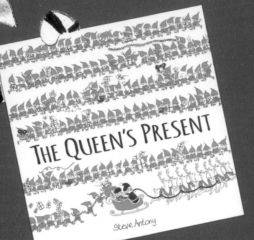
THE QUEEN'S PRESENT
Steve Antony

I'll Wait, Mr Panda
Steve Antony

Please Mr Panda
Steve Antony

THE QUEEN'S LIFT-OFF
Steve Antony

'This picture book is hard to beat.' The Times
THE QUEEN'S HAT
Steve Antony

GREEN LIZARDS VS RED RECTANGLES
Steve Antony

THE QUEEN'S HANDBAG
Steve Antony

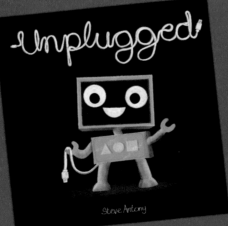
Unplugged
Steve Antony

For fun activities, further information and to order,
visit **www.hachettechildrens.co.uk**